THE DREAM PILLOW

Mitra Modarressi

ORCHARD BOOKS • NEW YORK

Orchard Books, 95 Madison Avenue, New York, NY 10016

Manufactured in the United States of America. Printed by Barton Press, Inc.
Bound by Horowitz/Rae. Book design by Mina Greenstein.
The text of this book is set in 16 point Cochin. The illustrations are watercolor reproduced in full
color. 10 9 8 7 6 5 4 3 2 1

Library of Congress Cataloging-in-Publication Data
Modarressi, Mitra. The dream pillow / Mitra Modarressi. p. cm.
Summary: Celeste and Ivy's friendship gets off to a rocky start when one gives the other a pillow that
induces bad dreams. ISBN 0-531-06855-2. ISBN 0-531-08705-0 (lib. bdg.)
[1. Nightmares—Fiction. 2. Dreams—Fiction. 3. Friendship—Fiction.] I. Title. PZ7.M7137Dr
1994 [E]—dc20 93-49400

TO MY MOTHER

Once there was a little girl named Celeste who lived next door to a little girl named Ivy.

You would think they'd be friends, but they weren't. They walked to school every day on different sides of the street, and when Celeste looked over at Ivy, Ivy looked down at the ground. Celeste thought Ivy must be very stuck-up.

One day Celeste had a birthday party and invited all her friends. She even invited Ivy, because her mother said she had to. Ivy came, but barely said a word to anyone.

Everyone brought presents. Ivy brought a soft velvet pillow that Celeste's mother said was very pretty. But Celeste thought anything that came from Ivy must have something wrong with it.

That night Celeste went to sleep and had a nightmare. She dreamed her little brother cut off all her hair.

The second night she dreamed she was buried under a pile of giant peas. She wondered why she was having so many bad dreams.

The third night Celeste
had a terrible nightmare,
about a family of monsters
who came to take her home
as their pet.

She woke up and began to wonder if the pillow was the
problem.

The fourth night she put the pillow in her closet and had no
dreams at all. So after that, she kept it there.

Some time later, Ivy had a birthday party of her own and
invited Celeste. Celeste wanted to bring a present as scary as
the one Ivy had brought her.

So she got the pillow out of the closet and sewed on a tail and
a face that made the pillow look like a cat. Ivy would never
guess that this was the pillow she'd brought Celeste.

Ivy was very happy to have a new stuffed animal and was especially nice to Celeste at the party. Maybe Ivy wasn't so stuck-up after all. Maybe she was just shy.

The two girls had a lovely time together. Celeste started feeling a little guilty.

That night, Celeste couldn't sleep. When she looked across the way, she saw a light come on in Ivy's room. She knew Ivy must be having a nightmare.

The next day in class, Ivy had circles under her eyes.

The day after that, she fell asleep in the middle of a spelling test.

And on the third day, she was absent.

Celeste worried that Ivy had been carried away by monsters.

Celeste felt she had no choice. She went to Ivy's house and confessed.

Ivy was astonished. She hadn't known the pillow caused nightmares. She said her mother had made it, so they decided to ask her about it.

Ivy's mother looked puzzled. She said she had followed her grandmother's recipe for a Daisy Delightful Dream Pillow, but perhaps she had put in too many daisies.

The magic needed to be cut in half. So Ivy's mother got out her sewing kit, took the tail and the face off the pillow, and divided it into two smaller ones with identical lace-trimmed edges.

That night, the girls had a sleepover. Celeste dreamed that she and Ivy had a tea party in a cozy little house made of an acorn.

Ivy dreamed that she and Celeste found two pairs of magic shoes that let them fly.

The next morning, they told each other their dreams over hot
cocoa and blueberry pancakes.

And from then on, Celeste and Ivy always walked to school together on the same side of the street.